What Kids Say About
Carole Marsh Mysteries . . .

I love the real locations! Reading the book always makes me want to go and visit them all on our next family vacation. My Mom says maybe, but I can't wait!

One day, I want to be a real kid in one of Ms. Marsh's mystery books. I think it would be fun, and I think I am a real character anyway. I filled out the application and sent it in and am keeping my fingers crossed!

History was not my favorite subject till I starting reading Carole Marsh Mysteries. Ms. Marsh really brings history to life. Also, she leaves room for the scary and fun.

I think Christina is so smart and brave. She is lucky to be in the mystery books because she gets to go to a lot of places. I always wonder just how much of the book is true and what is made up. Trying to figure that out is fun!

Grant is cool and funny! He makes me laugh a lot!!

I like that there are boys and girls in the story of different ages. Some mysteries I outgrow, but I can always find a favorite character to identify with in these books.

They are scary, but not too scary. They are funny. I learn a lot. There is always food which makes me hungry. I feel like I am there.

What Parents and Teachers Say About Carole Marsh Mysteries . . .

I think kids love these books because they have such a wealth of detail. I know I learn a lot reading them! It's an engaging way to look at the history of any place or event. I always say I'm only going to read one chapter to the kids, but that never happens—it's always two or three, at least!
—Librarian

Reading the mystery and going on the field trip—Scavenger Hunt in hand—was the most fun our class ever had! It really brought the place and its history to life. They loved the real kids characters and all the humor. I loved seeing them learn that reading is an experience to enjoy!
—4th grade teacher

Carole Marsh is really on to something with these unique mysteries. They are so clever; kids want to read them all. The Teacher's Guides are chock full of activities, recipes, and additional fascinating information. My kids thought I was an expert on the subject—and with this tool, I felt like it!
—3rd grade teacher

My students loved writing their own Real Kids/Real Places mystery book! Ms. Marsh's reproducible guidelines are a real jewel. They learned about copyright and more & ended up with their own book they were so proud of!
—Reading/Writing Teacher

"The kids seem very realistic—my children seemed to relate to the characters. Also, it is educational by expanding their knowledge about the famous places in the books."

"They are what children like: mysteries and adventures with children they can relate to."

"Encourages reading for pleasure."

"This series is great. It can be used for reluctant readers, and as a history supplement."

THE MYSTERY AT FORT THUNDERBOLT

by Carole Marsh

#3

Published by Gallopade International/Carole Marsh Books. Printed in the
United States of America.

Managing Editor: Sherry Moss
Cover Design: Rightsyde Graphics, Inc.
Illustrations: Brittany Donaldson, Savannah College of Art & Design
Content Design: Cecil Anderson
Cover image of Fort Pulaski courtesy of the National Park Service

Gallopade is proud to be a member and supporter of these educational
organizations and associations:

American Booksellers Association
International Reading Association
National Association for Gifted Children
The National School Supply and Equipment Association
The National Council for the Social Studies
Museum Store Association
Association of Partners for Public Lands

Gallopade International is introducing SAT words that kids need to know in each
new book that we publish. Look for this special logo beside each word in the
vocabulary section or glossary. Happy Learning!

Yoo-hoo is a registered trademark of Yoo-hoo Chocolate Beverage Corp.
Gulfstream Aerospace Corporation is a wholly owned subsidiary of General Dynamics.

a Word from the author

Dear Reader,

My granddaughter, Christina, and I like to speculate on "What if?" As you may know, I write mysteries set in real places that feature real kids as characters. The story is made up (fiction), but the fascinating historic facts are true (non-fiction). We are both often amused when readers guess "backwards" about what I made up and what is true in the books. Sometimes, I have a hard time being sure myself. Why? Because history is just as interesting and incredible as anything an author can make up.

So, one day, Christina and I were wondering: "What if a brother and sister had parents who worked in exotic places fighting dangerous new diseases? What if these two children stayed behind in coastal Georgia and spent a lot of time at an old Civil War fort?" It was easy to imagine a story that could be interesting, funny, scary, and feel real. But the truth is, Fort Pulaski has so much flabbergasting history that you have a big head start on a great story, no matter what you write about!

As I told Christina about the real fort and the surrounding area...its fascinating history as a slave trading center...what really happened at Fort Pulaski...the pirates who roamed the barrier islands...and the big old gators who roam the land today...well, it all seemed Pretty Darn Scary. I hope you, and Christina, think so, too!

Carole Marsh

Pretty Darn Scary Books in This Series

table of Contents

PROLOGUE

Do you think they see us?

No, I don't think they see us.

Do you think they hear us?

No, I don't think they hear us.

They look nice, don't they?

Yes, I suppose so.

No, really, they do. I think they must be about our ages when we—you know—when we...

Died, the word is died.

Yes, of course. Do you miss being, you know, alive?

I don't know. I don't remember.

I do. I miss it. They sure do seem real nice. She's pretty. He's kind, I think. But they seem sort of sad, don't you think? I wonder what's the matter. They spend a lot of time here. They just seem so sad sometimes. I think I'll get closer.

Mind your own business. Leave them alone. It's for the best. You know that, don't you?

Yes, I know. Still...

CHAPTER ONE

TELITHA

Telitha means "Morning Stars of the Water" in the Cherokee language. Telly, as she was called, was named that by her parents, both Bio Level Four employees of the CDC—Centers for Disease Control—in Atlanta, Georgia.

It was when they were first married. One of their early field assignments for the CDC was an outbreak of hantavirus on a Cherokee Indian reservation. The virus was deadly and it was killing the old people—the ones who still looked like real Indians—and the children, mostly infants.

One young orphaned girl, named Telitha, was strong and healthy. The new CDC doctors really believed that she would survive. But one night, she died of the disease. It really bothered the idealistic young doctors, who loved the science that had brought them to their unique careers, but who despised the pain and suffering, and sometimes horrid forms of death that they often witnessed in their jobs.

They never forgot the beautiful young Cherokee girl, and when their own daughter was born, just nine months later, they both knew what her name would be.

CHAPTER TWO

TIMBUKTU

Telly's younger brother, Tim, got his unusual name in a similar way. A couple of years after Telly was born, she had to stay with her Grandmother Wylly while her parents went on another dangerous assignment to a place called Timbuktu.

It was their first exotic medical emergency port of call, and they loved it. Working for the CDC was not like any other job. It was part doctor, part scientist, part spy. You had to be ready at a moment's notice to travel halfway around the world to try to put an end to a deadly outbreak of some dreaded—often incurable, and usually gross, horrid, and disfiguring—disease before it spread any further.

In the meantime, of course, you were at risk of being exposed to the disease. Even though every CDC field doctor took maximum precautions, things could happen. Contaminated air could be breathed. Needles could prick holes even in double layers of latex gloves. Sometimes CDC doctors became infected and died.

Telly believed that it was this "them against the disease world," as well as the drama and risk of their jobs, that appealed to her unusual parents. Timbuktu was their first really big case. And when their son was born they saddled him with the same name as this exotic, foreign place.

"What were you thinking?" Tim (for that was what he was called, naturally) would often demand after some bully found out his real name and hammered him unmercifully about it.

But Telly had noticed that in the last few years, Tim was less defensive about his name. (For the record, he thought Telitha was a beautiful name and wondered why his sister didn't use it instead of the boyish Telly.)

She noticed that sometimes when someone asked him his name, he responded with a curt: "Tim-buk-tu" in short, bitten-off syllables, almost as if he were challenging them to comment or tease. When he said his name this way, no one ever did.

CHAPTER THREE

THUNDERBOLT: TIM

"Hey, you gonna get Big Red and get my boat in?" A burly, sunburned man of about sixty asked the question in a demanding Yankee accent.

"You're next," Tim said flatly. He was respectful to those at the Thunderbolt Marina who were nice to him and his sister, who both worked there after school. He was never disrespectful to the rude ones, but he offered no apologies. They had to wait their turn like everyone else.

Thunderbolt Marina was in the town of Thunderbolt, an old fishing community on the ICW (the Intracoastal Waterway) which wound all along this part of the coast. A dashed line on nautical charts marked the ICW, a channel of water that boats could use to travel inland along the coast instead of going "outside," meaning in the Atlantic Ocean.

Any marina on the ICW was always busy, especially in spring or fall. In the fall, many boats traveled from colder states in the northeast down to warmer climes in Florida, or even on to the Bahamas. In the spring, the parade reversed itself and the boats scampered back to their home waters for the summer season.

All Tim knew was that lots of folks had boats, but not everyone actually knew how to boat. On the ICW you had everything from the big shrimp trawlers and long, skinny barges, to multi-million dollar motor yachts crewed by teams in matching polo shirts, to sailboats tall and small, to runabouts pulling skiers, and jet skiers buzzing around them all like bumblebees. It looked like fun, but it was always a chance for disaster, as well.

"Thank you," the courteous owner of the *My Girl* said, tipping Tim with a twenty-dollar bill.

"Thank you, sir," Tim responded politely. He had just used Big Red, the marina forklift, to hoist the forty-footer into the launch area. "Let me know if you need any help getting your gear aboard, sir."

The man nodded his thanks and moved on. Tim ducked his head so the surly Yankee who was frowning big-time would not see the slight grin he just couldn't help. Tim knew from the marine radio monitoring the water traffic that the guy had run his big, new powerboat aground on one of the shifting sandbars in the sound and had been too impatient to wait for the high tide to float it off. His impatience had cost him an expensive tow into the marina the day before.

Today, he was here getting his boat back out of the boat barn so some even more expensive repair work could be done. Tim marveled at how some boaters (with more money than sense, to his way of thinking) got GPS (Global Positioning System) and other electronic gear loaded on their boat, but failed to learn to use it before they actually set out on the water.

If they had asked, Tim could tell them the truth: the water was unforgiving of ignorance. Just ask Sea Tow, who hauled stranded or disabled boats in all the time. Or Coast Guard Station Tybee, nearby, which sent the orange helicopter called *Pedro*, as well as boats and men, to the rescue. Or, he thought, no sign of a grin on his face now, ask him and Telly, who had lost their younger brother a few years back in a stupid boat accident in the Savannah River within sight of land.

There was no place for stupid on the water.

"Your boat's ready, sir," Tim said to the Yankee man, who swigged back another beer and stomped toward the gangway to the dock, never bothering to acknowledge the courtesy.

CHAPTER FOUR

THUNDERBOLT: TELLY

"Your name sounds like a detective," the young boy teased Telly. "You know, the guy who used to eat Tootsie Pops on television. Or maybe you were named for tellyvision?" he guessed. "Or the tellyphone?"

Telly smiled and splatted some bubblegum pink paint at the boy. If you were a girl who worked at a marina, you had to expect teasing and even flirting from the guys. She took it in good nature, glad that she had a brother nearby just in case a teaser got too serious.

This was her favorite time of year. October on the Georgia coast was a big secret. All the tourists had gone back to school and work. But the locals loved this time of bright turquoise sky, cotton candy clouds, warm breezes, and the faint hints of autumn such as the green of the marsh grasses seeming to visibly seep away into the tea-colored water.

A breeze sluiced her long, blond hair across the top of her paint bucket and suddenly, she had bubblegum pink-fringed hair. The boy laughed and tossed her a piece of drop cloth. When Tim showed up about that time, the boy nodded to Telly and scampered off down the dock. No one really wanted to mess with Tim McKinnon, especially not when he was guard-dogging his older sister.

"Hey, Telly," Tim called, as he strode down the dock, his own blond hair glistening in the sun. "Decide to paint with your hair instead of your brush?"

Telly laughed. "Looks like it, doesn't it?" She swatted at her hair with the rag and stepped back. "Take a look; whatcha think?"

Her brother looked at the fresh new paint job on the back of the Sea Ray. CORINTHIAN it said in hot pink trimmed in black with some silver shading.

"Maybe when you grow up you can be an artist!" Tim said. He stood with his hands on the hips of his faded cut-off jean shorts. He thought his sister had a real talent with boat lettering, especially picking cool color combinations. Everyone loved her work, especially, as they always put it, since she was "just a kid."

Telly swatted the paint rag at her brother. "It's good. You know it is. Think Mr. Bailey will like it?"

Tim nodded. "It's perfect, Telly. He'll love it, only it's Captain Bailey now; he just got his license, I heard."

Scuttlebutt traveled fast on the water. "Good for him!" said Telly, meaning it. Like her brother, she loved the water, the boats, and seeing everyone enjoy both. But she admired people who went to the trouble to learn what they were doing before they went out. Even though she and Tim had been several years younger when their younger brother Georgie had died, she remembered the day clearly.

In fact, it would never leave her mind. Nor, as nearly as she could tell, anyone else's in her family.

CHAPTER FIVE

THE CALL

When Telly and Tim were finished at the marina, they did what they always did: they splurged on an ice-cold Yoo-hoo and sat in the white rockers on the dock before they headed home to do their homework.

Homework was no problem for them. "You studybugs sure got our genes," their Mom and Dad always said.

"It's not that," Tim disagreed. "We don't have a television in the house, you know? So, uh, there's not much to do after dark except homework."

It was true. The McKinnons were the only family they knew who intentionally did not own a television. Their parents said it had come about when they were both in medical school at Emory University in Atlanta. They didn't have any money to buy a TV, and besides, they had to study, study, study.

Telly and Tim never thought about it, having grown up without television, but they loved to give their good-natured parents a hard time about it anyway.

Their house on the salt marsh was a sprawling, sort of messy place with lots of wraparound porches, decks, and hammocks—perfect for book reading. The big, real-wood-burning fireplace drew them for reading and long-winded disease discussions, or shriekingly competitive games of Monopoly in the winter.

But ever since Georgie's death, their parents seemed to be gone more, even volunteering for distant assignments, especially when a fellow doctor had young children at home. The house was quieter, the games fewer.

Tim stuck to his computer, Googling one thing or another; Telly never knew what. And she focused on her art, or attempts at drawing. She and her brother lived on soup, sandwiches, and freshly-caught seafood from their dock. Friends, football, and the other usual school-age activities didn't play much of a role in their lives.

They were a bit too young to work at the marina, but the boss was their uncle and Mom and Dad liked that he kept somewhat of an eye on them after school. Tim and Telly liked earning a little money of their own.

"Time to go hit the books," Telly said, tossing her Yoo-Hoo bottle in the recycling bin, also part of their ritual before they headed home. She hadn't missed in 47 days.

Tim tossed his bottle and high-fived her as it slam-dunked into the bin. But when he jiggled in his rocker, she knew that their cell phone—set on mute—had vibrated. No one had the number except their uncle, whom they could see behind the counter writing up invoices, and their parents, who always waited to call them (no matter what time zone they were in) at home just before bedtime.

Well, at least no one else, except the CDC, which had never called. Ever.

Tim fished the cell phone out of his pocket. "Hello?" he said, assuming surely that it was a wrong number. But he stayed on the line, nodding. Frowning. Nodding. He hung up without saying a word.

"What?" Telly asked, almost certain that she did not want to know. They had been in a great mood all week because their parents were flying in this weekend from Zaire. They had promised that they would be home for an entire month, maybe even all through the holidays until the first of the year.

Tim did not speak for a minute. Then he finally said, "They're not coming home. Mom and Dad are not coming home this weekend."

Telly hated the look on his face and the sound in his voice. "Are they dead?" she asked. It was always a valid question.

Tim grabbed her hand. "Oh, no," he assured her. "But..."

"But what?" Telly demanded. What could be
worse than death? Why did Tim have this awful look on
his face? It gave her cold chills.

"They can't come home because they're in
quarantine," said Tim.

Their parents had been quarantined before. It
was a "big, inconvenient pain in the neck," as their dad
put it, but necessary when a doctor had possibly been
exposed to a disease.

"Tim..." Telly asked patiently, as if speaking to a
small child. "What is the quarantine for? What were
Mom and Dad exposed to?"

In a voice as quiet as a grave, her brother
answered: "Ebola. They've been exposed to Ebola."

Ebola, Telly knew, had no cure. No cure at all.

CHAPTER SIX

FORT PULASKI

Telly and Tim did not go home after all. They did what they always did when they were discouraged—they rode their bikes out to Fort Pulaski.

The fort was an amazing place. Partly because it was so historic. Partly because so much of it was still intact after almost 200 years. And partly, to Telly and her brother, because of its physical location on Cockspur Island looking out over the Savannah River right to the place where Georgie had died.

Fort Pulaski was named for the Polish hero who was mortally wounded during the attempt to raise the siege of Savannah in 1779 during the Revolutionary War. Telly thought his name—Count Casimir Pulaski—was quite dashing and romantic. She often daydreamed of a handsome count coming to her rescue—but her rescue from what she was never sure.

For some reason, when they were younger, Tim and Telly had begun to refer to the fort as Fort Thunderbolt. They had never dropped the nickname.

Before they set out for the fort, Tim explained that the CDC had said that all they knew was that a report had come in from Zaire that "the McKinnons" were under quarantine for Ebola. That the CDC should send two more doctors right away. And, that further information would be forthcoming as soon as some local tribe-versus-tribe fighting quieted down.

"Great!" Telly had said. "Just great. Mom and Dad may have a deadly disease, but they just might die of gunfire." It was amazing to her how many deadly germs seemed to favor remote locales, especially those in the midst of one civil war or another.

Tim had not bothered to tell his sister not to worry. They both were worrywarts—big time. If you ever lose someone you love, they guessed, you tended to worry a lot about those you still have. Or, the brother and sister earnestly hoped, they hoped they still had parents.

As they raced toward the fort, pedaling on the old oyster shell-encrusted railroad bed, it felt good to relieve their nervous tension, to hear the *crunch/crunch/crunch* of the shells beneath their tires, and to smell the salty scent of rising tide oozing its way into the tall, browning grasses.

With barely a wave at the park entrance station (the guards all knew the McKinnon kids and that they had season passes and practically lived at the fort), Tim and Telly strained against the pedals as they crossed the bridge over the South Channel and sped into the Spanish moss-draped entrance to Fort Pulaski.

They parked their bikes in front of the visitor center, and did what they always did next. They raced one another across the moat and demilune to the drawbridge. Usually Tim teased his sister that he was going to toss her to the alligators that swam in the moat, but this day he did not bother.

As always, they headed up the brick staircase to the terreplein, the upper level of the fort, covered with grass. They each mounted one of the cannons that stood atop the fort like beached Atlantic Right whales. From this vantage point, they could look out to sea and the Cockspur Lighthouse at the end of Lazeretto Creek.

A *lazeretto* (an Italian word for hospital) was located here in the mid-1700s. It was a quarantine station where new arrivals to the Savannah area were processed. Some of these newcomers to America were from Africa, black-skinned men, women, and children, kidnapped from their homeland and brought here to be sold as slaves.

Today, as usual, Tim and Telly thought about Georgie, but they also thought about quarantine and their parents.

"We have to do something, Telly," Tim said. "And we have to do it fast."

Telly glanced out at the little white lighthouse. "But what?" she asked. "Zaire is so far away. And we're just kids." To herself, she thought: Just like so long ago with Georgie; we were just little kids and couldn't help him either.

Tim just stared out to sea, his eyes the same steely gray as the Atlantic waters. "I'm thinking," he said. "I'm thinking."

CHAPTER SEVEN

See, I tell you, they are so sad. But they seem even sadder tonight. Worried too. Something's wrong; I can tell.

What's wrong is that you are paying any attention to them. They have their lives. We have ours.

Ha. Ha. I guess you were funny when you were alive too?

Yeah, I guess. I was just a kid, remember.

You and me both, Georgie, you and me both. I don't like the look in that boy's eyes. He's scaring me.

He's scaring you, Telitha? Now that is funny.

CHAPTER EIGHT

ACCUSED!

For awhile, Tim and Telly sat quietly. Since Daylight Savings Time had not "fallen back" yet, it was still light out on the horizon, although pink and purple streamers soon began to wave back toward the west.

Telly tried to imagine what it might have been like back during the U.S. Civil War here at the fort, which was considered invincible and "as strong as the Rocky Mountains."

Just a short time after the start of the Civil War (often called the "War of Brother Against Brother," Telly recalled), this federal fort was ordered to be seized. A great battle by Union troops at Hilton Head ensued against the Confederates at Fort Pulaski.

In an unfortunate blunder, the Confederates abandoned nearby Tybee Island. The Federal troops quickly took advantage of this mistake. They moved to Tybee—the only place where they could successfully bombard Fort Pulaski—and began their siege.

From more than a mile away, the Union soldiers were able to use their new rifled cannons to pierce the walls of Fort Pulaski, as if the bricks were brownies. When the damage was so great that the powder magazine was threatened, the Confederates were forced to surrender.

Fort Pulaski became a prison for some, a memory for others, and yet another example from history of how fatal it may be to assume "invincibility."

Tonight, as the stars began to appear, Telly thought about how cavalier her parents were to travel the world, darting right into the face of deadly microbes. Did they really think that their college degrees could protect them? Their big, fat biohazard suits? Double layers of latex gloving? Caution, even extreme caution? It only took a second. What had happened, she wondered? And what would happen to her and Tim if their parents died of Ebola?

"I've got it!" Tim said suddenly, snapping his fingers. As **agile** as a sea otter, he slid off the cannon and reached up to help his sister down as if he were in a great hurry.

"What?" asked Telly.

"We're going to do something," her brother said with determination. "And we're going to do it now!"

Telly was speechless as she slid down off the cannon. But she was even more speechless as they both watched the blue flashing light of a police car speed over the bridge and onto the fort grounds. When the wailing siren stopped, an officer hopped out of the car.

"I wonder who's in trouble?" Telly asked.

"I don't know and I don't care," Tim said. "We've got trouble enough of our own without worrying about someone else's."

When he tried to tug his sister by the arm toward the staircase, she **balked**. "Look!"

They stopped in their tracks and looked down to see their uncle from the marina jump out of the patrol car and frantically motion up at them. Likewise, the police officer waved a spotlight back and forth at them. He yanked a megaphone up to his mouth and called their names.

"Looks like we're the ones in trouble," said Tim with a frown.

"No, Tim!" cried Telly. "It must be about Mom and Dad! They must have some news. Let's go down. Hurry!"

Now it was Telly who pulled her brother along. One behind the other, they scampered down the brick staircase to the parade grounds below. Halfway across the drawbridge, their uncle and the police officer met them.

Telly looked at her uncle, but he never said a word. He just held one hand over his mouth, a helpless, troubled look in his eyes as the officer handcuffed first Telly, then her brother.

"You kids have been accused of the theft of the motor vessel *Haphazard*, kids," the officer barked. "Come with me."

CHAPTER NINE

AN ARRESTING DEVELOPMENT

In downtown Savannah at the Police Barracks on East Oglethorpe, Tim and Telly found themselves in a small room with a nice, lady detective, their uncle, and the Yankee man from the marina. Mr. Goldman was the owner of the *Haphazard*, the boat that Tim had put in the water earlier that day. Apparently, while the man returned to his vehicle to get all his gear, the boat had vanished from the dock. He had named Tim and Telly as the last people he had seen near his boat.

Uncle Benny explained over and over that Tim and Telly were just kids, underage, and in his care while their parents were out of the country.

Mr. Goldman explained over and over, "Someone stole my boat and I want satisfaction and I want it now!"

Telly and Tim would have been more frightened if they hadn't been so worried about their parents.

To them, this was just a ridiculous accusation and a big inconvenience since Tim was eager for them to get on with his plan.

Finally, the exasperated detective said, "Mr. Goldman, you will just have to be patient. Go with the officer here and he will take your statement and your information." The man looked very flustered and disgusted to be dismissed like that, but he had no choice but to follow the officer to a different small room.

When they left, the woman laughed. "Well, there's yet another person who thinks that how things were done 'back home' is better than how we do them here. But I have a feeling that Mr. Goldman would find the same justice there as here, considering the circumstances."

"The circumstances?" Tim asked.

The woman, Detective Norris, patted Telly's quivering hand. "We just had a report from the Coast Guard that a boat matching the *Haphazard's* description was found aground and sinking off McQueens Island."

"So he grounded his boat again?" asked Tim. "He was drinking at the marina, and I know that he does not know his GPS from his..."

Detective Norris interrupted him. "Oh, it's worse than bad boat driving," she explained with a serious look on her face. "Even as we sit here, Mr. Goldman is being indicted on insurance fraud. We don't believe he wanted to get his boat out of the Thunderbolt Marina boat barn so he could get it repaired from its previous mishap."

"He wanted to wreck it so he could get money and buy a new boat?" Telly guessed.

Uncle Benny sighed. "And blame my niece and nephew? That's some pretty dirty pool."

"Yes," agreed the detective. "I'm sorry for the inconvenience, but his original complaint was valid, so we had to bring you in to ask some questions. I'm just glad the boat was found that quickly."

"Me, too," said Tim. "Telly and I have urgent things to do."

Uncle Benny gave him a suspicious look. He loved these kids and they were good, but so unsupervised. He wished his sister and her husband would just come back to Savannah and be ordinary doctors. Of course, if he had known about the phone call from the CDC, he would have been more suspicious.

Instead, he just asked nervously, "What's so urgent?"

Telly and Tim exchanged glances. "Homework," said Telly. "We have tests tomorrow."

It was true, but they would not be at school to take them.

CHAPTER TEN

HEAD TO SEA

After Uncle Benny whisked them by Tubby's Tankhouse for some takeout seafood, he dropped the kids off at their house. A lone, lonesome light glimmered in the window. He felt sorry for these kids. It was almost like they were orphans.

"You sure you guys will be ok?" he asked, as Tim and Telly hopped out of the car.

"Sure, Uncle Benny, thanks," said Tim. It was dark now and he could see the bluish circles hanging under the man's eyes. He'd never gotten an education like his older sister, their mother. Marina work was all he knew and it was dawn to dusk and like tonight, always headaches.

"Thanks for the seafood," Telly said and gave her uncle a kiss on the cheek. "We'll be fine. Homework. Bed. No TV, remember?"

In spite of himself, Uncle Benny laughed. "Your parents, they just won't do, will they?" He, himself, was headed home to his trailer to watch Monday Night

Football and eat his takeout, and probably fall asleep in his chair. He usually did, after all.

But when both kids seemed to freeze at the mention of their parents, and Telly even tear up, he paused. "You sure you guys are ok? I mean that police station thing. I'm sorry. If I get my hands on that Goldman..."

The kids came back to their senses. "Then we'll be back at the police barracks," Tim warned with a grin. "Just drop it. I have a feeling Mr. Goldman won't be boating again anytime soon."

Uncle Benny nodded, yawned, and gave his niece and nephew one last look. "Well, ok. Lock up now, and don't stay up too late. Promise?"

Telly looked at her brother. She didn't want to lie to her uncle. He was a sweetheart and good to them.

"Promise," she heard Tim agree.

As their uncle drove off, and Tim unlocked the door, Telly gave him a quizzical look.

"I didn't lie," he said. "If things work out we won't stay UP too late. We will lie DOWN."

Inside, Telly checked for phone messages. There were none. She didn't know if that was good or bad. She picked up the cell phone Tim had left on the counter and shook it, as if that might make it ring. Might make Mom or Dad call and say everything was ok. Everything had always been ok before. But this felt different.

During many of their after-dinner talks, their parents had regaled them with facts about diseases that could make you "bleed out" from every orifice in your body. They'd eaten dessert over discussions of diseases that could cause your body parts to fall off. The excited way their parents talked, it was like blood and gore was the most fascinating thing in the world. And to them, it was.

Tim and Telly appreciated how smart their parents were, how much in love because of their shared talents and interests. They valued how their parents tackled the **daunting** task of saving lives against the unknown on a deadline.

But sometimes it was hard not to resent being left alone so much, being left out of the action, so to speak, and when they were home, talking about everything but the heartbreak they all held inside like some festering, incurable disease: Georgie.

"Pack us two small duffel bags," Tim ordered his sister. She had never heard such a tone in his voice. The sense of urgency scared her. "Gather any money you can find around. Leave a note for Uncle Benny that we're ok, that we'll be back."

Telly looked at her brother in the dim light. "Will we?" He didn't answer the question. "I'll be on the computer," he said. "Hurry."

Telly did as she was told. Even though she was older, Tim was often the man with the plan. She knew he did not mess around. If he thought this was a good idea, she trusted him. She just wished that she knew what the idea was.

When the duffels were packed, she went to find her brother. He was on the Georgia Ports Authority website. When she tried to look over his shoulder, he shut down the computer. "I'm ready," he said. "Let's go."

As they passed through the kitchen, Telly grabbed the cell phone from the counter.

"Leave it," Tim said. "It might give us away."

"But how can we hear about Mom and Dad?" Telly pleaded, near panic. "This is the only phone number the CDC has. It's the only way Mom and Dad can reach us if we're not home, Tim!"

Before Tim could answer, Telly was further astounded when a taxi pulled up at their door. "I called it," Tim said sheepishly. "We don't have time to ride our bikes."

"Ride our bikes to where?" asked Telly. But Tim was out the door and Telly had to race to catch him.

"Where to?" asked the taxi driver, as if school age kids called him at midnight all the time.

"Fort Thunderbolt," said Tim. When Telly punched him in the side, he quickly corrected. "Fort Pulaski, and don't waste any time, *please*."

CHAPTER ELEVEN

What are they doing here?

I don't know. The fort is closed for the night.

The fort's never closed for the night to us.

No, but they should be home in bed. What's up?

What do you care?

I don't know, I just care. Isn't it ok to care, even if we are dead?

Sure, I guess.

That boy, he favors you.

Don't say that.

So does she, his sister.

I said, don't say that.

I don't see why not? They're good-looking kids.

Yeah, whatever.

Well, let's just watch. Let's listen. Ok.

Sure, yeah. Why not?

CHAPTER TWELVE

A MAN WITH A PLAN

Neither the kids nor the driver said a word as the taxi sped beneath the yellow flashing lights of Thunderbolt and revved over the arc of bridge that spanned the ICW. In the beam of the annual Hunter's Moon (so called because the Indians hunted by the bright light), shaggy palm trees quivered in the breeze like restless beasts.

The tide was turning, the kids could smell it. You couldn't live around the coast for long and not unconsciously pick up the rhythm of the sea. The human body became a barometer, able to sense, perhaps from a slight change in blood pressure, the change of tides. The scent on the wind told you things, much as sailors can smell land from a distance.

The yellow cab with its checkerboard paint job pulled up to the chained entrance to the fort grounds. The cabbie took his fee and tip and nodded. Perhaps from years of experience of minding his own business, the kids felt confident that he would not call any authorities to tattle that some crazy youngsters were marauding around the fort after hours.

As he drove off and turned onto the highway, Tim and Telly were left in the eerie darkness that only 25 million handmade bricks piled into a massive edifice...the shadowy waters of a reptile-filled moat...and ghostly drapes of Spanish moss can give.

Without a word, Tim cut left and scampered through the scrub into the fort. Telly followed, ducking under limbs he held until she passed. She knew gators moved about at night and worried about a close encounter of the bloody tooth kind. But Tim moved so quickly, she just tried to keep up.

When they broke out into the light again, Tim paused, then headed across the demilune to the drawbridge. The hulking black cannons seemed to aim their dark eyes directly at the trespassing children.

Tim opened the knapsack he'd brought along and plucked out a rope tied to a barbed hook and a pair of crampons like mountain-climbers use. Telly gasped as her brother attached the spiked metal to his shoes. He gave her a mischievous grin as he tossed the rope up over the gorge wall.

"Wait here by the door," he said, and before his sister could object, the boy began to haul and climb his way up the sally fort wall.

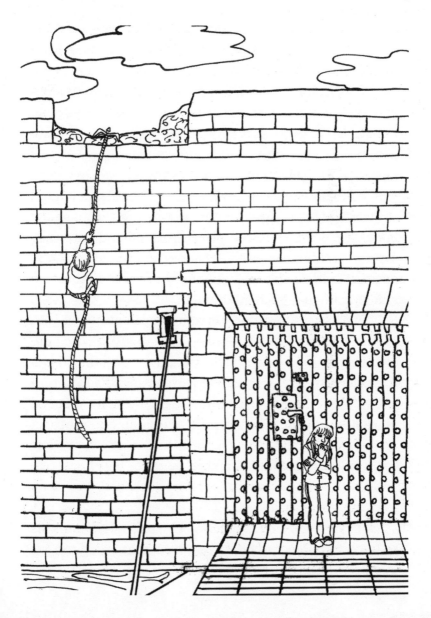

For the first time, Telly was afraid. The air grew chill. In the distance, the **cacophony** of night bugs rattled out a song. Slate gray clouds scudded across the moon, as if it were closing its eye to this misdemeanor. A splat and eddy of water in the moat made her cringe. Involuntarily, she sucked her toes deep down into her socks.

Before her loomed an enormous wooden door studded with bolts as big as fists. She knew that behind the fort door stood a large, wooden grille called a portcullis. The criminal term "breaking and entering" flitted through her mind. Then she giggled and said aloud, "Yeah, that usually means picking a lock with a credit card, not tackling something designed to keep tens of thousands of soldiers at bay."

It was then that she heard the noise. It was faint, but nearby. It sounded like a girl. It sort of sounded like an echo of Telly's giggle, but there were words too. Soft words. She couldn't make them out. One voice sounded more like a boy's. She spun about, but saw nothing.

CHAPTER THIRTEEN

ENTER IF YOU DARE!

Just then, Telly heard a boy's voice she recognized. She spun back around toward the fort door.

"Move back!" she heard Tim warn. And as she took a cautious step backwards, the drawbridge began to quiver as the portcullis screeched upward and the fort door creaked open just far enough for Telly to slip through.

She came face to face with a red-faced Tim, winded from his trek over the wall and effort to get the fort door open. Quickly, he closed everything back the way it had been.

Even in the dark of the sally fort, Telly spotted a strange look on her brother's face. "What's wrong?"

Tim stuffed his gear back into the knapsack and rubbed his eyes. "Nothing," he said. "I just thought I saw something."

"What?!" asked Telly in panic. Was someone else in the fort this night? Did he mean an animal? Was there a guard?

"Not like that," Tim assured her.

"Not like what?" Telly asked, confused.

Tim stood up and stretched. "Not...not like something real. Just something. Maybe wispy. Maybe white. I don't know. I think I need glasses, or something. The light's probably playing tricks on my eyes."

Telly coughed. "What light? It's dark in here!"

Tim ignored her. "Come on. Time's a'wasting. We have to get up on the parapet."

"Why?" Telly begged as she ran after him. "Tim, you have to tell me what's going on! What are we doing here?"

"On top," he hissed back at her. "On top."

Exasperated, Telly followed.

Moonlight carpeted the brick staircase. Telly thought about all the trouble this fort had seen. She and Tim had been in every nook and cranny, either on school field trips or during their many visits here together.

She knew that beneath them were the parade ground, living quarters, jail cells, yucky toilets where the men had just stuck their bottoms out of holes in the wall to do their business in the moat. In her mind, she could imagine the hot days with the Savannah humidity and the mosquitoes as big as dinner plates.

Her teacher had explained the poor quality of food, often infested with weevils. The sour water. The rats, spiders, snakes, and, of course, the gators.

When it was bitter cold, the soldiers, often young and inexperienced, suffered most. The dankness. The disease. Yellow fever had been prevalent in these parts. The ancient local cemeteries were filled with those of all ages who had died of the dreaded disease. There had been no CDC or doctors like their mom and dad to fight that enemy back then.

Mom and Dad. Mom and Dad. Telly tried to climb, not think.

When they got to the grassy area on top, Tim scampered over to the parapets on the east wall and stared out to sea. He seemed satisfied not to see anything and sat down and gulped a swig from a water bottle attached to his belt. He held the bottle out to his sister who plopped down beside him.

"I think I heard something," Telly said, as she sat down and took the water.

Frantic, Tim glanced behind them.

"No," Telly said. "Back on the drawbridge."

Her brother looked doubtful. "What? What did you hear?"

"I don't know," Telly admitted. "It was soft, quiet. But it sounded like a boy, and a girl. I think one giggled." When her brother looked at her like she was crazy, she added, "Really, Tim. I heard something."

Tim frowned. "Don't worry about it," he advised. "Just help me keep a lookout." He motioned toward the lighthouse.

"What are we looking for?" Telly asked.

"Joe Bibbs."

"Joe Bibbs?! What..."

Tim interrupted her. "He's bringing his boat. I e-mailed him from the house. When he gets close, we're going to meet him. He's going to take us out in the channel."

Telly couldn't believe what she was hearing. "Why? Why didn't he just pick us up at the dock at our house? Or the marina?"

"Because," Tim said, with a rare aggravated tone in his voice. "Because we need to get to a certain spot in the channel when it happens. We have to be in place. Joe monitors the port traffic marine channel."

Telly stared at her brother in the darkness. His face was as clouded over and unreadable as the moon. "What place? Where? Why?"

Tim pointed to a spot just offshore. "There," he said. "The freighter *Iksalup* will pass there at 9:20. That's where the pilot boat will meet her so the pilot can board the ship to take her out to sea."

"So what?" said Telly, accustomed to the ever-present coming and going of the enormous container ships. "What does that have to do with us?" Then she grew quiet.

Just then, Telly felt sure she heard the voices again. One sounded worried. One sounded angry. She could hear their intent, but not the actual words.

Suddenly, Tim swatted at his eyes.

"What is it?" Telly asked. "What's wrong?"

"Nothing," Tim said. "I just thought I...never mind!" he interrupted himself. "There it is! The light! There's Joe—let's go."

Before his sister could argue, Telly was tugged up from the ground and hustled to the very edge of the high eastern fort wall. Tim attached the hook to the parapet and yanked at it. It dug in tight. Next, he attached a rope tied to his waist around his sister's waist.

"Get in front of me," he ordered. "Don't look down. We're just going to rappel real slow and easy. It's not that far, really."

Once more, before Telly could complain, she found herself moving slowly down the wall. The brick scraped her hands until she quickly learned to keep them free and just touch her feet to the wall as Tim moved them down the wall via the rope.

It was frightening each time he swung them out a few feet and they slid down the rope...and just as frightening each time she saw the wall heading toward her and the jerk as they touched...bounced...swung out into darkness...and then finally—with a gasp by them both—plunged into the moat.

Just as they hit the water, Telly was certain she heard a cry. She did not think she had made the sound—she was too scared to speak. Nor did she think it was Tim, but then she did hear him.

"Swim!" Tim cried. "It's just a little ways."

Telly did. They were both good swimmers. But the water was dank and cold and she knew its resident gator was somewhere. Even worse, the only thing to swim to was another wall—a sheer brick cliff with no way for Tim to haul them up.

CHAPTER FOURTEEN

JOE BIBB

As planned (though it would have been nice for her brother to tell her, Telly thought), just as they reached the far wall of the moat, a light shone down on them. It was Joe Bibb. He inched the flashlight beam out of the startled kids's eyes and tossed down two ropes.

Joe was a big and brawny fisherman who hauled trawl doors in on the shrimp trawlers, so it was no problem for him to pull two lanky kids out of the water and into the marsh. He handed each a small, fish-smelly towel.

"We ain't got much time," Joe warned Tim. "I brought the *Henrietta* in as far as I could. She's just over there. Come quick and watch out for water moccasins and gators." He turned and stalked off.

When Telly gave a small squeal, Joe turned and gave her a grin. She could see his big white teeth glow, even in the dark. She liked Joe. He was a real

Thunderbolter, been here forever, fished rain/shine/heat/cold/lightning/thunder—a real "no excuses" guy. Tim had a way of attracting good friends like this. She knew a lot of people felt sorry for the "McKinnon kids" with their crazy Disease Doc parents. That's what Joe called them. "Heard from the Disease Docs?" he'd always ask when he came around the marina.

Soon they had stamped their way through the marsh grass to Joe's ratty little runabout, *Henrietta*. He helped both kids onboard, climbed on himself, and the dinghy never even rocked.

When Joe started the powerful Johnson motor, the noise startled them both. Tim pulled his sister down onto a bench seat and they held on as Joe shoved the throttle forward and the boat skimmed through the narrow channel that only an old salt like Joe could navigate in the dark.

Telly tried to ask her brother more questions, but she could not be heard above the din of the motor. When she saw him turn and stare back at the fort with a puzzled look on his face, she mouthed "WHAT?" at him. Her brother just shrugged his shoulders and stared ahead into the night.

When they got into the South Channel, Joe slowed the boat to an idle. As they chugged past the little white Cockspur Lighthouse—a pale birthday candle in the darkness—Telly reached for Tim's hand. He did not pull back, but gave her hand a gentle squeeze.

It had been five years since their little brother Georgie had died in this spot. He'd been swimming merrily just off the sandy beach as the rest of the family picnicked nearby. Suddenly a jet ski had raced out from nowhere and run Georgie down. The man had been drinking. He was going flat out and had thought he could make the turn, but he hadn't—or at least not far enough out to miss the young boy.

Telly recalled as clearly as if it were daylight how her parents had jumped up when they saw the boat coming, fast and out of control. Telly and Tim had called to their brother and jumped up too. But it was too late.

Later, Telly remembered her parents crying softly night after night at the dinner table, after they thought Telly and Tim were asleep.

"If only he'd had a disease, we could have helped him, we could have saved his life," their Dad had groaned in dismay.

Mom had just cried.

It was not long after the funeral when their parents had begun to sign up for more and longer and much farther away field assignments. Telly knew she and Tim could—maybe should—be resentful. But they were a smart family and sensitive; they saw that grief took a long time and many strange turns.

It was a relief when Joe swung the bow out toward the channel. He said nothing. He knew the story and had graciously allowed these kids to have their private moment of mourning. But suddenly, he shouted: "Hear that?!"

None of them could have missed it. It was the deep, haunting *NNNNNNGGGGGGGGGGHHHHHHHH* of a freighter's horn. (All of Savannah slept to that mournful moan.) Truly, instead of pestering, it was a comforting sound. It was the sound of ships plying the seas, to and fro, on peaceful missions of commerce, versus the pirating or war battle days of yore.

"Should be the *Iksalup*," Joe said, and neither Telly nor Tim doubted his experienced judgment. "I'll get us in position," he added with a nod to Tim.

Slowly, Joe moved *Henrietta* on a convergence course with the enormous freighter, a castlelike hulk so large that from the viewing vantage of water level, it blocked sight of much of the sleeping town and the taut spaghetti strands of the Herman Talmadge bridge.

"Tiiiiiim?" Telly began, now suspicious. "And just exactly what are we getting 'in position' for?" When her brother did not answer, she repeated more demandingly, *"Tiiiiiiim?"*

He turned to her. "We're going to board the *Iksalup*," he confessed. "After they take the pilot on

IKSALU

board, Joe's arranged for us to go up the ladder, too.
I think he bribed a crew member," he admitted.

Telly looked totally confused. She could not
imagine boarding the gigantic vessel by climbing the
swinging, swaying rope ladder high up into its hull. But
even more, she could not understand why they would do
this. Then, suddenly, she did.

"And just where is the *Iksalup* headed?" she
asked her brother in such a stern voice that he knew
that she knew the answer already.

And yet, he answered. "Zaire. The *Iksalup* is
bound for Zaire."

CHAPTER FIFTEEN

I don't like this. I don't like this at all.

That doesn't really matter, does it?

But what are those two kids up to? I fear for them. I think it's dangerous, whatever they are doing. And who was that guy who met them at the moat?

I have no idea.

Can't we follow them? Can't we help?

No, you know very well that we can't. What do you think we are, their guardian angels?

Maybe. Maybe we are. Have you ever thought about that? Who said we had to stay here at this lonesome, forlorn fort forever? No one! I say let's head to sea with them. Let's help. Let's do something!

You can't swim.

Ha, ha. What difference does that make?

Well, from my experience, not much. I was only five and I could swim real good. Real good. Lot of good it did me though. Stupid drunk jet skier.

Don't be so bitter.

Why not? Why aren't you? You died, too. Who saved you?

No one could. They tried. I told you that story. But maybe we could try. Maybe we could help. Those kids, they sure do look like you a lot. I think there's something you're not telling me, Georgie.

CHAPTER SIXTEEN

THE

IKSALUP

Zaire, Telly thought. Where their Mom and Dad were, or at least she guessed that's where they still were. Dead, dying, or alive, she had no idea. She felt like she should know, like she should be able to feel the facts of the matter in the marrow of her bones. Bones, speaking of which, were growing colder and stiffer out here on the water, waiting...waiting...waiting.

The next thing Telly knew, the *Iksalup* was upon them: a dark shadow on the dark water. Her horn blared again—*NNNNNNGGGGGGGRRRRRRR*—and Telly shrank from the sound so close that it seemed to overpower them, to actually blanket them, even go right through them. She could hear the echo of the blast retort across the water, back from the dark buildings of the city, back from the all-encompassing night itself.

"Standby," Joe whispered, holding the rudder tightly. Idling steady in the *Iksalup's* stern shadow, they watched the pilot boat come about and the pilot haul himself up the rope ladder into the port passageway and vanish.

Just then, a flashlight clicked on and off from that same passageway, quick, just a blink. It was aimed right at the *Henrietta*. Telly didn't know whether to be afraid or relieved that they'd been discovered. But that wasn't it at all. It was the signal.

"That's your cue!" Joe cried. There was no sense worrying about being quiet. The drone of the *Iksalup's* engines masked any sound on the water.

The pilot boat left a sparkling wake as it headed back to Savannah, oblivious to the drama unfolding behind it. Joe shoved their duffels at them and held the rope ladder tight. Up above, a dark silhouette motioned for them to hurry.

"Thanks, Joe, thanks a lot," Tim said.

"No problem," answered Joe. "Be careful and good luck." Tim nodded.

As usual, Telly had to go first. Chilled and tired, she grabbed the rope ladder with both hands and stuck one foot on a slippery rung. As she lifted her other foot, a gust of wind caught the ladder and swayed her dizzily back and forth.

"Keep going!" her brother urged, as he and Joe tried to hold the ladder tighter.

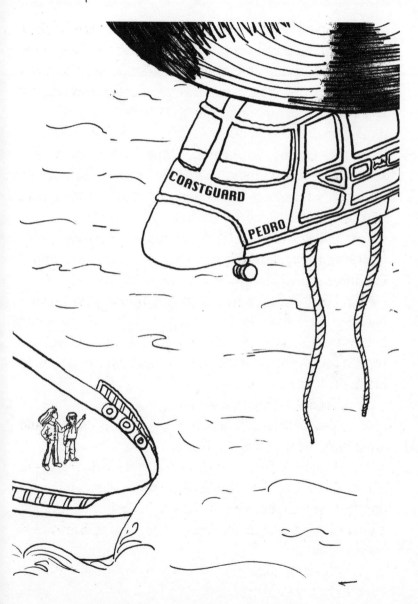

Once she had climbed a couple of rungs, Tim started up behind her and the extra weight held the ladder a little steadier. Still, it seemed strange and dangerous to hang from the side of a freighter the size of a twenty-story building, in the dark, from a skinny, sliver of cord.

Up and up they climbed until a dark arm in a jumpsuit grabbed Telly, then Tim, by the arms and pulled them up onto the platform that led into the ship's hull.

Just as Telly could finally breathe, she was both stunned and blinded by a sudden enormous orb of light. The light was so bright that none of them could even see the helicopter it was attached to, but they could hear it:

"HALT! STOP WHERE YOU ARE! THIS IS THE U.S. COAST GUARD. YOU ARE UNDER ARREST!"

And so for the *second* time that night, Telly and Tim were hauled down to Savannah's police headquarters!

CHAPTER SEVENTEEN

SOME EXPLAINING TO DO!

"Um, hm," muttered the pretty detective, the same one who had processed them before. *"Ummmmm, hmmmmmm."*

Telly and Tim sat frozen to their chairs—partly because they were still cold from their breezy whisk downtown via helicopter, and partly because they were afraid of what might happen next. There was no Yankee boater to blame this on. They were guilty as charged.

The detective tossed her brown curls as she read the arrest document: "You are charged with illegally boarding a seagoing marine vessel, the *Iksalup*, headed for the country of Zaire. What do you have to say for yourself?"

Tim sat silently, his arms folded over his chest. He stared down at the brown metal table. It was clear that he wasn't going to talk.

But Telly figured that if they were going to find their Mom and Dad they couldn't do it from a jail cell. She spoke up: "We were just desperately trying to get to Zaire anyway we could," she explained.

The detective let out a disgusted chortle. "Uh, what? There's a school field trip to Zaire? Goin' on vacation? Are you part of some television reality show?" She chortled again.

This made Telly angry. Her face flushed as she looked Detective Norris straight in the eye and said, "Really, I'm afraid it's pretty much the last one—*reality.*"

And when the detective looked both puzzled and curious, Telly explained about their parents and their jobs at the CDC and the phone call that they'd had about them being quarantined in Zaire for a disease called Ebola. Tim squirmed the whole time Telly talked.

The detective gave a big sigh and sat down. "And this Ebola is...?"

Tim snapped his head up, placed his hands spread-eagle on the table, leaned forward into the detective's face and said, "Ebola destroys the human immune system. If infected you get a high fever, an ugly rash, and sooner or later, you bleed-out."

"Bleed-out?" repeated the detective.

"Bleed internally and externally through every hole in your body," said Tim. "There is no vaccine and no cure."

"So could your parents possibly have survived?" Detective Norris asked gently.

Tim looked at his sister and shrugged his shoulders. "Antiviral drugs can help, but they might have all been used during an epidemic in a war zone. The death rate ranges up to ninety-percent."

No one spoke.

Suddenly they all turned when the metal door screeched as Uncle Benny slipped into the room. He wore baggy jeans with his pajama shirt tucked inside. The officer who had brought him down tipped his cap to the detective and left.

"Uh, hi, kids," Uncle Benny said tiredly. "Thought you were going to bed?" Without asking the detective, he pulled out a chair and with a yawn, sat down.

Detective Norris cleared her throat. "It seems that your niece and nephew thought that they might be able to get to their parents in Zaire as stowaways on the *Iksalup*," she said sternly, looking at the kids, not their uncle.

Uncle Benny perked up. He swiped his balding head. "Oh, yeah? Stowaways?" Instead of being upset,

he acted like that was something he could get behind, or
perhaps, had done himself in his younger years. His
glazed gray eyes seemed to be looking deep into
the past.

Finally, he caught the detective's squint and
straightened up. He waggled his finger at the kids in
admonishment. "Bad idea, kids," he said, as if
reprimanding a pet, "bad idea. You could get in trouble
like that."

"*Ahem...*" said the detective. "They ARE in
trouble." When she saw the forlorn look on the face of
the children, she softened her tone. "But I can see why
they would try so hard to get to their ailing parents."
With a sigh, she confessed, "Who could blame them?"
She, too, had a faraway look in her eyes.

For a moment, the room was quiet except for the
hum of an ancient air-conditioning unit. The silence was
startlingly broken when the detective snapped her
fingers loudly, red nail polish flashing. "I might have an
idea!" she said. "How would you kids like to stowaway
on something a little faster than an ocean freighter?"

CHAPTER EIGHTEEN

A QUICK TRIP

While the detective got on the phone to make all the arrangements, Uncle Benny, now caught up on the dire situation, drove Tim and Telly to their house to wait for Detective Norris' call.

But when they entered the house, the brother and sister had only one thing on their minds: the cell phone. They raced to grab it, but when they got to the kitchen table, both froze as if afraid to pick up the phone and find what? That there was no message? That there was one? Either seemed a fearful consequence.

Before either could retrieve the phone, it shocked them all by ringing. As it rang, it skittered across the table from the vibration like a confused lab rat.

Tim grabbed it first. "Hello?" he said hesitantly.

Telly and her uncle held their breath as Tim just listened and nodded. At last he said in a dejected tone, "Thank you. It's ok."

Telly could hardly open her mouth and squeak, "What?" It had been twenty-four hours since the first message. She had no idea when her parents might have been infected with Ebola. She couldn't recall, offhand, the incubation period.

Finally, Tim said, "It was the CDC. They say that all communication is still cut off from Zaire because of the civil war. No word on Mom and Dad. They could have been moved out of the country, or they could still be there. They said they would let us know something when they knew."

Telly sighed, disappointed at the news, yet relieved that it was not the worst news that they could have received. "It doesn't matter," she said. "Soon, we will be on our way to them."

Uncle Benny yawned. He glanced at his battered, old watch. The kids didn't even think the watch still worked; it was just a reflex, a habit of his. "I think you kids should pack your bags and get a couple of hours sleep."

Telly gave her uncle a hug. "Well we think you should go home and go to bed. Detective Norris is picking us up in a few hours, so you might as well go home and rest."

"Yes," Tim agreed. "There's no sense you staying up all night. We'll be ok."

Their uncle looked doubtful. After all, he had retrieved them from the police station twice in the last few hours. Still, he gave them a relieved hug. "I'll be by the phone," he said. "Be careful, you two."

The kids accompanied him to the front door and waved as he drove off in his beat-up pickup truck into the darkness. As the single red taillight faded into the night, they felt utterly alone.

"I can't sleep, can you?" said Tim.

"No," said Telly, "and we don't need to pack a bag—we still have our duffels. I don't think I can stand to just sit here a couple of hours waiting to leave."

"Me either," said Tim. He grabbed the cell phone off the table and stuffed it in his jacket pocket. "Come on."

"Where are we going?" Telly asked, surprised.

Her brother shrugged his shoulders as if to say *Where else?* "Fort Thunderbolt," he said.

CHAPTER NINETEEN

A BIKE RIDE

Instantly, they were on their bikes and pedaling down the highway as if chased by ghosts. Telly had to admit that it felt good to "get physical"...to do something besides spin their wheels, to wait, to worry worry worry and feel so helpless.

The wind had picked up and thunder rumbled out toward Tybee Island. They could just see the Tybee Light flashing in the distance. Pink lightning flickered on the horizon. There was no more sign of the moon.

At the fort, they hid their bikes out of sight and slipped through the same sliver of brush. As always, the sprawling fort greeted them with long open arms of brickwork. Telly wondered if that was why this was such a retreat for them—it was always here. A fortress for the heart. A sanctuary for lost souls.

This time, fortunately, Tim had no intention of scaling the sally port wall. "Let's just walk around her," he said, "then we'll head back."

Telly nodded and they traipsed along the grassy surround, staying well away from the edge of the moat. As she knew they would, as they always did, when they got to the point where they could see the Cockspur Lighthouse, they stopped. The small, squatty lighthouse was just a stub on the small island. It was mid-tide. And, as always, the memories of their younger brother and the day that he died washed over them. Only this time it was different.

For the first time, Telly could ever recall, Tim spoke of Georgie. "He was a cute little bugger, wasn't he?"

A knot caught in Telly's throat. She smiled in the darkness, glad Tim couldn't see the tears streaming down her cheeks. "Yeah, he was adorable. He loved to follow you around, remember that?"

Tim coughed, as if he had a choke of his own. "Yeah, and he loved to teethe on my shoelaces. You'd think he was half kid, half puppy."

Telly giggled. "Well you know, it is the job of the younger brother to be a pest," she teased.

"Gee thanks," said Tim. For a moment he was quiet. Then he asked in a soft voice. "Do you think Mom and Dad loved him best?"

Now it was Telly's turn to be quiet. "Yes," she finally said. "Yes, I think they did." And then in a moment, she added, "Wouldn't you?"

Tim reached down in the darkness to retie his shoes. "Yes," he agreed at last. He sighed loudly. "Hey, you know how I know they loved him best?"

Telly was truly perplexed and a little afraid to ask. "No, Tim, how?"

"It's plain as day," Tim said, something he usually said when he was about to pull a fast one on his sister. "They gave him an ordinary name: not Telitha, not Timbuktu, but George. Just George. Whoever started calling him Georgie, anyway?"

Telly laughed. "You, silly. You were learning your letters when he was born and you were on G. So you always called him George-G, because Mom and Dad said his name started with a G."

"Georgie," Tim said softly.

"Georgie," repeated Telly, even softer.

The wind had picked up even more, the thunder a louder grumble and the lightning closer. "I think we'd better head back," Telly said.

As they turned to race around the fort back to their bikes, Tim asked, "Heard any ghosts tonight, sis?"

"No!" Telly called back over her shoulder. "Seen any, little brother?"

"Not a one," Tim admitted.

As they scampered through the brush and retrieved their bikes, a huge bolt of lightning struck nearby. The vivid light lit up the fort with a pink glow.

"Hey, speaking of names, maybe this is why we always called this Fort Thunderbolt?" Tim said.

"I think so, Tim," said Telly, and she raced ahead of him, trying to stay in front of the storm hurtling their way.

CHAPTER TWENTY

STOWAWAYS

They barely made it back to the house in time to park their bikes and retrieve their duffel bags before a police car pulled up out front and flashed a quick blue light.

Detective Norris gave their damp hair a suspicious look and said, "I called. You didn't answer. Buckle up. We need to get to the airport fast before this storm comes in. We're really pushing it."

The kids noticed that the detective looked tired and windblown, but mostly she looked determined as she stared straight ahead into the first fat drops of rain. As she turned onto Victory Drive, the long view of tall palm trees, planted in memory of World War II veterans, loomed before them like soldiers on parade.

When the first traffic light glowed red, Detective Norris said, "Aw, what the heck!" and the car's sirens blared and blue lights flashed. "It's time for everyone to get up for work anyway."

The kids giggled in the back seat. But as the car sped through the remaining night, they grew quiet and sober.   Outside of watching the storm, there was nothing else to do but sit and worry.

The detective seemed to know a shortcut. Instead of taking the interstate, she roared up MLK Boulevard and onto the road that led by the Wildlife Preserve known for its large number of gigantic alligators.   Mom and Dad used to take Tim and Telly there when they were younger. The gators had been so many and so large that in some places they were piled up like cords of wood.   Once they had seen a large white wood stork eat a baby alligator with the gator stuck in the bird's neck for a long time—its outline clearly visible through the white feathers.

Telly had asked how the alligators knew that they were supposed to stay in the preserve.   Dad had just laughed and said, "You better watch where you walk in Savannah, kiddo!"

Just thinking of this made Telly stare hard out her window just in case a twelve-footer decided to amble across the highway tonight.   She wanted nothing to get in the way of their getting to Savannah/Hilton Head International Airport in time.

Which they did, but it didn't matter.

CHAPTER TWENTY ONE

STORM!

As the patrol car screeched out onto the tarmac, a figure in a bright yellow rain slicker flagged them over to a hangar. Detective Norris whipped the car into the hangar. "Stay put!" she barked to the kids in the back seat as she jumped out.

Tim and Telly watched nervously as the detective and the man talked rapidly, waving out toward the worsening weather and the sleek Gulfstream airplane with its engines running and its propeller spinning in the rain.

"This doesn't look promising," Tim groaned.

Telly couldn't stand the thought of them not getting away. The plan was to head for Charleston, South Carolina where they were to unofficially board a military cargo aircraft headed for Zaire on a humanitarian mission. "Stowaways," the detective had said, but Telly knew she had pulled strings for them to get to hitch a ride. But if they couldn't get to Charleston...

At last Detective Norris bolted back into the car. She turned to the kids. "Well, it looks iffy, I'm afraid to say," she told them. "However, the pilot is monitoring the weather channel and they expect a break in this storm soon. So hang tight, because if it comes, you'll need to make a dash for the aircraft. Got all your gear?"

Simultaneously, Telly and Tim held up their duffel bags. Telly knew that they were ready to get to their parents, gear or not. She didn't really want or need anything right now except her mother and father. She gazed at the cell phone her brother held. If only it would ring with news—good news.

Suddenly, the man in the raincoat gave a big wave and Detective Norris shouted, "Now! Let's go!"

They all dashed out of the car. The raincoated man grabbed each kid by an arm and turned to hustle them out to the waiting aircraft.

"Stop!" Detective Norris screeched.

They all stopped in their tracks and spun around. Telly was afraid that the detective had changed her mind about letting them go. Instead, she gave them each a big, bear hug. "Good luck!" she cried, and they could not tell if those were raindrops or tears scrolling down her cheeks.

The man frowned and the detective nodded and let go. Before the kids could say anything, he was all but dragging them to the plane, where another raincoated man practically pushed them by their bottoms up the steps.

Once aboard, the pilot, not looking up, ordered: "Take your seats, buckle up, we've been cleared for takeoff."

Hurriedly, the children did as they were told. And as if by magic, the rain abated and the clouds suddenly cleared a path. Telly grabbed her brother's hand and said, "We're going to make it!"

But Tim could hear nothing over the roar of the engine. The pilot muttered into his headset. The instrument panel of lights in front of him flickered and changed. Suddenly the door flopped open and the co-pilot, drenching wet, climbed aboard.

"So glad you could make it," they heard the pilot yell at him.

"I was in bed asleep," the man snarled back. He turned and gave the kids a menacing look.

"With your dog?" asked the pilot with a grin, holding his nose.

Reluctantly, the co-pilot grinned back. "No."

Then instantly, they turned to the matter at hand.

GS 191, YOU ARE CLEARED FOR TAKE-OFF ON RUNWAY ONE A, THAT'S ONE ALPHA. WEATHER WINDOW TIGHT. TOWER, OVER AND OUT.

TOWER, THIS IS GS 191 PROCEEDING TO RUNWAY ONE ALPHA FOR TAKE-OFF. PLEASE ADVISE IF ANY CHANGE. GS 191 OVER AND OUT.

And then, the Gulfstream made a graceful turn...the engines roared louder...the blue lights of the runway came into view...and the fuselage quivered as they sped up into the last of the night.

As the aircraft lifted off, Telly breathed a sigh of great relief. She saw her brother do the same.

Once more, the pilot muttered into his headset. The co-pilot/engineer seemed busy with hand motions. They both leaned forward and stared into the dimness where the rain was revving up once more.

Over the din of engine and rain, the children heard the unbelievable:

TOWER, TOWER THIS IS GS 191 RETURNING. PLEASE CLEAR FOR LANDING. WATERSPOUT SPOTTED. WE ARE COMING AROUND. PLEASE ADVISE.

And after a sputter of static:

GS 191, YOU ARE CLEARED FOR IMMEDIATE LANDING. SPOUT SPOTTED ON RADAR. WINDSHEAR ADVISORY; REPEAT: WINDSHEAR ADVISORY. USE RUNWAY B2. PLEASE RESPOND.

The pilot was curt: *B2.*

And as tears trickled down Telly's cheeks, and

rain streamed down the small porthole windows, the airplane, bumping and jogging in the wind, bounced to a safe landing.

As he maneuvered the plane toward the hangar, the pilot turned. "Sorry, kids. Looks like a no-go indefinitely."

CHAPTER TWENTY TWO

WHAT NEXT?

"What next?" Tim mumbled into his collar as he and his sister sat waiting for the pilot and co-pilot to complete their post-landing checklist.

In the hangar, Telly could see Detective Norris with her hands clasped to her cheeks at the unfortunate turn of events. Telly figured that she would take them home and, well, that would be that. They would go back to staring at the cell phone. Finally, the door was opened and the co-pilot, with a sorrowful look, helped the children out. He pointed across the tarmac to the hangar and the kids made a run for it. No one helped them this time. They were on their own.

Instead of awaiting them with open arms, as they expected, Detective Norris made a dash for the patrol car. Before the kids were even halfway to the hangar, she had started the car and sped out of the hangar past them. As the car passed, she did not even look at them. She was hunkered over the steering wheel staring straight ahead.

Tim and Telly were speechless. They slowed from a run to a somber walk. There seemed no point to hurry. By the time they got to the hangar, they were drenched. There was no one there anymore. They turned in time to see the pilot and co-pilot making a dash for the terminal. And then, the hangar lights, on a timer, they supposed, went out.

Telly and Tim stood there in the darkness. Alone.

CHAPTER TWENTY THREE

A FINE HOWDY-DO

"Well, this is a fine howdy-do," snarled Tim. He shook the silent cell phone fiercely. "What are we supposed to do now?"

Telly wiped her eyes and sighed. "I don't know," she admitted. "I guess we can try to get home. Maybe the weather will clear later."

Tim's laugh was one of devastation. "Oh, yeah? So what? Do you see anyone here concerned about the weather, or us, or our Mom and Dad? Do you?"

Telly cringed. "Please don't be so discouraged, Tim," she begged. "Mom always said that it's darkest just before the dawn."

Her brother stared out into the rain. "That's what I'm afraid of," he said softly.

"Huh?" said Telly.

Tim turned to his sister. "Didn't you hear what you just said?" When Telly looked puzzled, he said, "You said *said*. You said Mom *said*. That's the past tense, Telly. That's what they say about Georgie when we overhear them talking about him late at night—that is, when they're ever home. They say Georgie *said* this, or Georgie *said* that. *Said* is what you say when someone is dead, Telly."

Telly grabbed her brother by the arm. "That's not how I meant it, I promise, Tim," she swore. "I meant Mom *says*...Mom *says* that it's always darkest..."

At that moment, they were jolted by the sudden and unexpected ring of the cell phone. In spite of the noise of the rain on the tin roof of the hangar, the phone sounded exceedingly loud.

Tim pulled away from his sister's grasp and answered. He listened only a moment and then hung up.

Telly did not like the look on his face. "What?" she asked, her voice and her now chilled body quivering.

"They said wait right where we are."

"Who said?"

"I don't know."

In a daze of dread, the two children peered out into the darkness. It was foggy now, so no matter who had called, it certainly wasn't to say that they were about to fly.

For awhile they saw nothing. Then in the ghostly mist they spotted the eerie orbs of blue light from the patrol car. It was moving very, very slowly.

As the car approached, Tim and Telly squinted at the headlights. Soon they could see the face of Detective Norris. She was peering through the fog, her bottom lip clenched between her teeth.

And then behind her, they saw a tall man with a stern look on his face. He was dressed in a navy blue military uniform, the brass gleaming in the fog like gold beneath waves of water. He stood very erect and strode somberly and purposefully toward them.

Telly froze, certain this was the news that they had dreaded. There would be no other reason for the slow pace of the car, the reason for official military personnel, or the grim look on Detective Norris' face. She glanced over at her brother. He had his head down, eyes closed, hands clasped behind his back. It was the posture of acceptance.

And then, the pink of dawn pierced the far sky. In an instant, it spread out along the horizon, the bright sun shoving up the curtain of dark storm clouds, so bright, that for a moment, the children were blinded.

But as the pink spread, two new figures appeared, but only in black silhouette against the baby blanket sky. It was the pilot and the co-pilot. Each pushed a wheelchair ahead of them. In each chair sat a person wrapped in a blanket from head to toe. Only a tiny pale face peered out from each of the white cocoons.

"Mom," Telly whispered.

Tim's head shot up. "Dad," he said.

And then both children were running, running toward the dawn.

CHAPTER TWENTY FOUR

DAWN

Telly and Tim stared at their almost unrecognizable parents. Their mom, always thin, looked like she'd lost twenty pounds. Her ashen face was tired and wan. Their dad also looked thinner. His face seemed unnaturally yellowish, as did the whites of his eyes. He seemed weak as a kitten and both of their voices were soft, as if it was exhausting to speak.

"Are you ok?" Telly asked, afraid to even touch them; they looked like they might shatter and break.

"We're out of danger," their father said. "We're going to be ok. It just might take a while for us to regain our strength."

"So you really did have Ebola?" Tim asked, meaning if so, then how did you survive. The death toll in the village was now at eighteen, according to the CDC.

Their mother shook her head slowly. "We don't know what we had for sure; the lab work is still being done. But it was bad, real bad." She hung her head.

When Tim still looked confused and dissatisfied, Dad said, "We think it might be a strain of Ebola. Plus we are young and healthy enough, perhaps, to have been able to fight it off...eventually." He looked pained to recall the experience.

"We're sorry we didn't call," Mom said. "During the outbreak, the village also had a civil war. All communications were cut off. We got one email to the CDC which called you, but after that, everyone could only hunker down in the hospital there and try to survive." She looked apologetic.

"Oh, Mom," Telly said, "it's ok. We were just so worried. We tried to get to you, we really, really did." Her arms slapped her sides as if to mean what could we do, we're just kids. Behind them, the military man, the pilot, the co-pilot, and the detective smiled.

"How *did* you survive?" asked Tim. He and Telly exchanged glances and she knew that they were thinking the same thing: their Mom and Dad had survived because they were together; they had survived for each other. And so, what was said next truly startled them.

"You," said Dad with a wan smile. "You are why we survived."

When the brother's and sister's mouths both fell open, their mother gave a weak little laugh. "It's true," she said. Tears welled in her eyes. "When the meds ran out and we could do no more than lay there and wait, I would look at your father and mouth *Tim.*"

"And I would look at your mother and say *Telly,*" added Dad. "We said it over and over and over."

Their mother sniffed and wiped a tear. "Sometimes—in our delirium—we said *Georgie,*" she confessed.

Now Telly and her brother exchanged new looks. In her heart, Telly knew that she and her brother had always felt third in line for her parent's love after their love for one another and the love for their long, lost baby son, Georgie. But now—it hit her like a thunderbolt—they knew the real truth: their parents loved them just as much.

"YOU saved our lives," said Dad, more strongly. "You didn't even have to be there, so that's pretty good doctoring."

"Oh, Mom!" said Telly.

Her mother spread her hands. "We're not contagious, you know," she said, and her daughter dashed into her arms.

Tim fell into his father's embrace and suddenly, they were all laughing and crying and blubbering, "I love you."

When their mom and dad had to sit back, Telly said softly. "Mom, if it makes you feel any better, I think Georgie is okay." And when her parents looked puzzled, she added with a smile, "Really, I do."

Tim cleared his throat. "You know," he said with a blush. "I've been thinking. Maybe I'll go to medical school and become a CDC doctor like you guys. I remember when I was a kid and you helped that Indian village during the hantavirus outbreak. That was pretty cool."

Their mom and dad exchanged curious glances. Tim and Telly wondered what they were thinking.

"Well," Dad said, "that would be fine, son. We would be proud of you, but you know, your mother and I have been discussing something, and we think we will spend more time in Savannah. In fact, we were thinking of opening a business so we could spend more time with you guys."

"A business?" said Telly, stunned.

"What kind of business?" ask Tim, with a doubtful look on his face. Doctoring was all his nerdy parents knew how to do.

Once more their mom and dad exchanged glances and smiles. "Why, a marina, what else?!" said Mom. "We thought we'd buy out Uncle Benny. He's asked us before if we would like to own the Thunderbolt Marina, and we think we would."

"Uh..." added their father. "You kids know any good after-school dock workers?"

Tim and Telly laughed, **ecstatic** at the idea.

Detective Norris interrupted. "Has anyone noticed that it's pouring rain again?"

The McKinnon family looked at her. All together they answered, "No."

POSTLOGUE

Boy, it's good to see them back, isn't it?

Yeah, I guess.

Yeah, you guess? You are glad to see them; admit it.

Yeah, you're right, I am.

They look a lot happier, don't they? Much more relaxed. I wonder where they've been and what they've been up to?

I guess we'll never know.

Well, maybe if we listen, instead of talk talk talk.

You know, you're funnier than you used to be. You seem happier yourself. And you know what else? You still favor them. How do you explain that?

I think some things just don't need explaining.

Yeah, I guess.

THE END??

about the Series Creator

Carole Marsh is an author and publisher who has written many works of fiction and non-fiction for young readers. She travels throughout the United States and around the world to research her books. In 1979 Carole Marsh was named Communicator of the Year for her corporate communications work with major national and international corporations.

Marsh is the founder and CEO of Gallopade International, established in 1979. Today, Gallopade International is widely recognized as a leading source of educational materials for every state and many countries. Marsh and Gallopade were recipients of the 2002 Teachers' Choice Award. Marsh has written more than 30 Carole Marsh Mysteries™. Years ago, her children, Michele and Michael, were the original characters in her mystery books. Today, they continue the Carole Marsh Books tradition by working at Gallopade. By adding grandchildren Grant and Christina as new mystery characters, she has continued the tradition for a third generation.

Ms. Marsh welcomes correspondence from her readers. You can e-mail her at fanclub@gallopade.com, visit the carolemarshmysteries.com website, or write to her in care of Gallopade International, P.O. Box 2779, Peachtree City, Georgia, 30269 USA.

built-in book Club
talk about it!

Questions for Discussion

1. What did you think when you first read the prologue to the book? Did it make you want to read more to find out what was going on?

2. Would you want to be a doctor or a nurse who works at the Centers for Disease Control? Why or why not?

3. Have you ever ridden in a boat? If so, what did you like about it? Was there anything you did not like about it?

4. How would you like to grow up in a home without a television? What would be some good things? What would be some bad things?

5. Do you like to visit historic places like Fort Pulaski? Why or why not?

6. What did you think about Tim's idea to board a container ship going to Africa? Did you think it was a good idea or a bad idea? Why?

7. Why do you think doctors leave the comforts of the United States and go to foreign countries to work?

8. Why did Telly and Tim think that Georgie was their parents' favorite child?

9. What was the most interesting thing you learned about Fort Pulaski and Savannah, Georgia? Would you like to visit the area?

10. Talk about some of the jobs in this book, like a pilot, ship captain, police detective, and a doctor. Which one would you most like to have when you grow up?

built-in book Club
bring it to life!

Activities to Do

1. Build a sailboat! You will need construction paper, scissors, and glue. Start with a 6-inch by 3-inch piece of paper. On one long side, cut off the corners. Add a small rectangle for a cabin on top of the long side you did not trim. Create a mast using a 1/2-inch by 6-inch strip of paper. Glue the mast behind the rectangle. Behind the mast, add a right triangle for the sail. The triangle should be big enough to go from the top of the mast to the bottom of the mast. You can attach a small flag at the top if you wish!

2. Picture it! Do you remember when Telly and Tim rapelled down the fort wall and landed in the moat? Draw that scene. Don't forget that Telly was afraid of alligators in the water. Maybe you can add some

little alligator eyes watching them from the water in the moat!

3. Get the facts! Do some research about Fort Pulaski. When was it built? Why was it built? Who was Casimir Pulaski, and why was the fort named after him? What happened when Fort Pulaski fell to the Union Army in 1862?

4. Map it Out! Find a map of Georgia and a map of the United States online. Print each one. First, mark the locations of Savannah and Fort Pulaski on the Georgia map. Color the map. Next, locate Georgia on the United States map. Color Georgia red. Find the state where you live. Color it blue. Finally, draw a route from the state where you live to Georgia. How many states do you cross?

5. Have a seafood feast! Telly and Tim enjoyed seafood that they caught from their dock. Ask your parents to help you make some tasty seafood dishes like shrimp, crabcakes, or fish filets. How about some hush puppies and coleslaw on the side for an authentic Southern-style feast? (Aren't you getting hungry just reading this?)

Pretty darn Scary
glossary

agile: moving with quickness and ease

balk: to stubbornly refuse to move or act

biohazard suit: loose, one-piece garment worn to

protect against germs or chemicals

cacophony: loud, confusing, disagreeable sounds

daunting: intimidating; discouraging

demilune: triangular piece of land protecting the rear

wall of Fort Pulaski

ecstatic: feeling great delight

marina: a place where boats can dock

microbes: microscopic living organisms including viruses and bacteria

parapet: a protective wall over which defenders of a fort fired their weapons

quarantine: isolation of someone who is carrying a disease

tech
Connects

Useful Websites to Visit

Check out these websites for more information about the Okefenokee Swamp!

On Fort Pulaski...
www.nps.gov/fopu

On Centers for Disease Control and Prevention...
http://www.cdc.gov/

About Tybee Lighthouse...
http://www.tybeelighthouse.org/

About Georgia...
http://www.georgiaencyclopedia.org/nge/Home.jsp

More resources
Fort Pulaski and the Defense of Savannah
(Part of the National Park Civil War Series)

enjoy this excerpt from...

The Ghosts of
Pickpcket
Plantation

by Carole Marsh

CHAPTER ONE

his name was telesphore

HIS NAME WAS TELESPHORE. He had no idea why his grandmother had named him that. His grandmother had to name him because his mother had died giving birth to him. His father was nowhere to be found. No name had been selected, not even hinted at, much less batted about from some charming book of baby names. So his grandmother named him Telesphore. Thank goodness his friends called him Terry. But somehow, deep underneath, he felt like Telesphore, a name that seemed auspicious, but also a burden. But he couldn't think of that now. Now he had to think of snakes.

Water moccasins were part and parcel of the peat bog swamp that surrounded Pickpocket Plantation. So were alligators. Mosquitoes the size of saucers. Wild turkeys. And, rarely, a wild boar.

"Watch where you s.....t......e......p," Terry reminded himself. His Aunt Penelope had lent him a beat-up old pair of hightop, lace-up boots, but he figured a diamondback rattler's fangs could easily pierce right through the leather as if it were butter. Terry realized that he had involuntarily squiggled his feet so far back up into his shoes that his toes were cramping. "Step carefully," he whispered to himself.

Terry wondered how anyone had ever gotten anything done going tippy-toe around the enormous plantation acreage. "Shoot," he said aloud, again to himself, "I will just stomp along like brave Huck Finn might have done and take what comes." As he walked more willfully, he tried to recall if Tom Sawyer and Huck Finn had been more brave, or cowardly. Either way, they were on the Mississippi River, and Terry did not think alligators the length of small cars had ever worried them, except perhaps in their imaginations.

In Terry's imagination, he was scouting out Pickpocket as it must have been in the days of the Yamacraw Indians, or in the painful era of plantation slavery, or during the wily time of the Civil War (the War of Northern Aggression, as some old-time southerners still called it), or some other time of historic excitement. But, really, Terry knew in his heart that he was just trying not to be bored.

Or scared. After all, didn't Aunt Penelope say that the Saturday *Savannah Pilot* recently featured a story about a fisherman poling his skiff through some snarled morass of wetland weeds getting his foot chomped off by a gator?

   "Step carefully, Terry...

      c   a   r   e   f   u   l   l   y."

enjoy this excerpt from...

THE SECRET OF EYESOCKET ISLAND

by Carole Marsh

#4

CHAPTER ONE

A STRANGE FATHER

Daniel Brickhill was a strange father. His wife had died giving birth to a boy and girl, twins. Therefore, he had been destined, as a man of honor and duty, to raise these children, though he knew nothing about children or childrearing. The children, Simon and Frederica, did not care about these things; they loved their strange father dearly.

Daniel Brickhill was a fisherman; he had been so all his life. He could, and would (indeed, must) fish anytime and anyplace to make a living to support his family.

The Brickhill family lived in a typical ramshackle cabin in a small fishing village near the south end of the Altamaha Sound. This was his children's home, but this was not his home. His home was the sea, or the sounds, or the tidewater creeks—wherever fish schooled, or shrimp ran, or crabs congregated.

Dan Brickhill's former home had been on the outskirts of London, England, where he awoke each day to the deep-throated *bonging* of Big Ben. He and his own strange father, also a widower, had lived in a similar fishing village. After just a few years of school, young Dan had joined his father on the docks and set to sea to fish the fish; it was the only life he knew.

However, Dan Brickhill knew that his children would not fish for a living. He knew this because he had promised their mother this as she had asked him, gasping, on her deathbed. And Dan Brickhill never broke a promise, most especially not to his beautiful, dying young wife.

And so, his children attended the local Buttermilk Sound School each day, faithfully, and did their homework faithfully by lantern light each night. They were bright students, eager to learn about the world beyond. That their father was illiterate was irrelevant to them—he was still the smartest man that they knew, or, so they believed, that they ever would know.

When they offered to teach their father to read and write, he scoffed, "No need! Them fish don't read, so no need me learnin' how to scrawl a note and stick it on a hook. You kids just learn for you and me both, and your mother, of course."

Because Dan Brickhill fished from dawn till dusk, and often slept overnight on trawlers at sea when the fishing was good, Simon and Frederica spent much of their time in the cabin alone. This was not a problem since they both knew how to cook, wash their clothes, clean the cabin, and study hard. But it was lonesome.

Their father feared this simple existence lacked some essential survival skill he believed that his children needed—indeed, that everyone needed, even in spite of the more newfangled life he knew was lived on the mainland—and this disturbed him greatly.

And so, on the first day that school was out for the summer that year, he devised an educational plan of his own. And a very strange plan it was, indeed!

WRITE YOUR OWN MYSTERY!

Make up a dramatic title!

You can pick four real kid characters!

Select a real place for the story's setting!

Try writing your first draft!

Edit your first draft!

Read your final draft aloud!

You can add art, photos or illustrations!

Share your book with others and send me a copy!

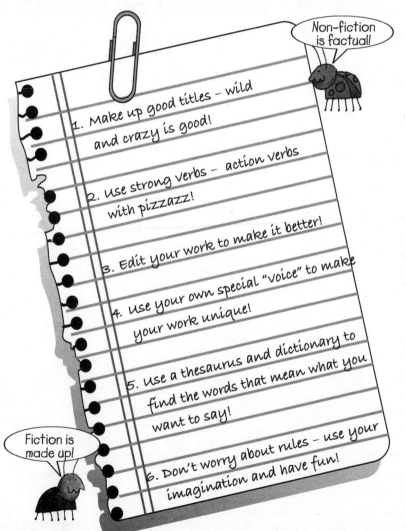